116

THIS BLOOMSBURY BOOK
BELONGS TO

....

For Grandad Jack, Aunty Jacqueline and Uncle Andy –
for all the special memories

First published in Great Britain in 2001 by Bloomsbury Publishing Plc
38 Soho Square, London, W1D 3HB
This paperback edition first published in 2003

Text and illustrations copyright © Stephen Waterhouse 2001
The moral right of the author/illustrator has been asserted

A CIP catalogue record of this book is available from the British Library

ISBN 0 7475 5579 6

Printed in Belgium by Proost

3 5 7 9 10 8 6 4 2

GET BUSY THIS CHRISTMAS!

Stephen Waterhouse

BLOOMSBURY
CHILDREN'S
BOOKS

The penguins love Christmas, and can't wait to get busy preparing all the Christmas treats!

Each year...

They SING Christmas carols LOUD and PROUD...

They carefully WRAP everything up...

They CUT DOWN two great big trees!

One for OUTSIDE their igloo...

MERRY CHRISTMAS

One for INSIDE their igloo!

They COOK nice, tasty food...

And then the party begins!
They EAT the delicious food...

They OPEN their presents with lots
of excitement...

They PARTY with lots of energy, late into the night!

And then they are so tired...

They fall FAST ASLEEP!
HAPPY CHRISTMAS, penguins!

Enjoy more great picture books from Bloomsbury ...

FIVE LITTLE FIENDS
Sarah Dyer

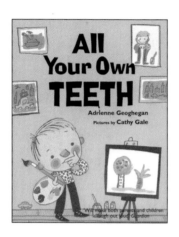

ALL YOUR OWN TEETH
Adrienne Geoghegan & Cathy Gale

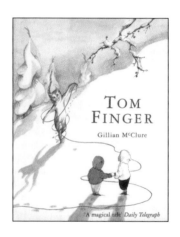

TOM FINGER
Gillian McClure

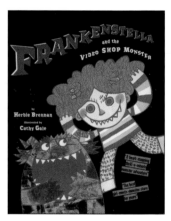

**FRANKENSTELLA AND THE
VIDEO SHOP MONSTER**
Herbie Brennan & Cathy Gale